For José,
who was, is, and always will be
my best friend.

BLOSSOM AND BOO

by Dawn Apperley

British Library Cataloguing in Publication Data

A catalogue record of this book is available from the British Library.

ISBN 0 340 81764 X (HB)

ISBN 0 340 81765 8 (PB)

Copyright © Dawn Apperley 2001

First edition published 2001

10 9 8 7 6 5 4 3 2 1

Published by Hodder Children's Books,

a division of Hodder Headline Limited,

338 Euston Road, London NW1 3BH

Printed in Singapore

Blossom and Boo

A Story About Best Friends

Dawn Apperley

Hodder
Children's
Books

Blossom and Boo were best friends. Every day Blossom met Boo, and together they would go to play in the woods.

In the summer, the sun shone and crickets buzzed. Blossom and Boo went exploring. "It's a swinging tree," yelled Boo.

They sat in the flowers and made each other presents.
"They're friendship crowns," Blossom said, smiling.

Blossom and Boo walked by the stream.
"Let's splash stones," said Boo, giggling.

Blossom made a little *splash*; Boo made a little *splosh*. Then together they made a big *SPLASH* and an even bigger *SPLOSH*.

In the autumn, leaves turned golden, fiery colours.
  "It's berry time," said Boo. "Let's have a picnic."
  Blossom and Boo collected the berries deep in the woods.
But Blossom fell down and hurt her paw on a thorn.
Boo bandaged her paw with a leaf and held her tight.
Soon Blossom felt much better.

Blossom and Boo were enjoying their feast, when some mice scampered off with Boo's berries. Boo started crying.

"Why are they being so mean?" he asked.

"Some animals just aren't very nice, Boo," said Blossom, putting her arm around him. "Here, have mine," she said, and she gave him the rest of her berries. And Boo felt much better.

Soon, the trees in the woods started to lose all their leaves and the birds flew away for winter. Boo became sad.

"Soon, I won't be able to play with you," said Boo, snuffling.

"Why?" asked Blossom.

"I have to hibernate in winter," said Boo.

"What does that mean?" asked Blossom.

"I have to sleep for a long time," explained Boo.

Blossom knew she would miss Boo lots.

"You will still be my best friend," said Boo, "even when I can't play with you every day."

"You will still be my best friend, too," said Blossom, sniffling.

Blossom and Boo snuggled up in the glade, and the falling leaves tickled their noses. They both got the giggles. And then Blossom and Boo weren't that sad anymore.

Winter had almost arrived. It became dark much earlier in the woods now.

"I'm afraid of the dark," Blossom said, trembling. Boo held her paw.

"Look at the big, bright moon," Boo said, smiling. Together they looked at the shining moon and twinkling stars. And Blossom didn't feel so scared anymore.

One morning, it was very cold in the woods. Snow was falling and it was very quiet.

When Blossom went to Boo's cave, Boo didn't come out to play. Blossom waited . . . and waited . . .

"Boo! It's me!" shouted Blossom in her very loudest rabbit voice. But still Boo didn't come out to play. He was fast asleep.

Every snowy day, Blossom went to Boo's cave.
But Boo didn't come out to play. So Blossom had to play
in the woods by herself. She was very sad and lonely.
She missed her best friend.

But when Blossom went to the field
she remembered the friendship crowns.
And when she went to the stream
she remembered the splish-splosh stones.
And when she hurt her paw she remembered the special leaf.
And when she went to the glade
she remembered getting the giggles.
And when it became dark and scary
she remembered to look at the moon.
And when she remembered all these things,
she smiled because she remembered her best friend
and she felt better.

It was becoming warmer in the woods. The first flowers were blossoming, and the trees had little leaf buds. Spring was finally here!

One day, Blossom was watching the birds come back
to the woods when she heard a BIG, LOUD yawn.

"Boo!" cried Blossom happily, hopping into his arms. Boo had woken up from his long winter sleep. Blossom and Boo had the biggest best-friend hug in the world!

Then they marched off into the woods to do all of their favourite things...together!